ORCA
Echoes

SAM'S RIDE

BECKY CITRA

Illustrated by AMY MEISSNER

ORCA BOOK PUBLISH

Library and Archives Canada Cataloguing in Publication

Citra, Becky
Sam's ride / Becky Citra ; illustrated by Amy Meissner.

(Orca echoes)

ISBN 978-1-55469-160-9

I. Meissner, Amy II. Title. III. Series: Orca echoes

PS8555.I87S24 2009   jC813'.54   C2009-904581-8

First published in the United States, 2009
Library of Congress Control Number: 2009932874

Summary: Sam overcomes his fear of horseback riding and comes to appreciate
both his grandfather and life on the ranch.

Orca Book Publishers gratefully acknowledges the support for its publishing programs
provided by the following agencies: the Government of Canada through the Book
Publishing Industry Development Program and the Canada Council for the Arts, and the
Province of British Columbia through the BC Arts Council
and the Book Publishing Tax Credit.

Typesetting by Teresa Bubela
Cover artwork and interior illustrations by Amy Meissner

ORCA BOOK PUBLISHERS
PO Box 5626, STN. B
VICTORIA, BC CANADA
V8R 6S4

ORCA BOOK PUBLISHERS
PO Box 468
CUSTER, WA USA
98240-0468

www.orcabook.com
Printed and bound in Canada.

12 11 10 09 • 4 3 2 1

To my brother John,
for his great enthusiasm about my books.

CHAPTER ONE
SAM'S SURPRISE

"Please…please, Mom, don't make me stay here," said Sam.

Sam and Mom were sitting at the table in Grandpa's kitchen. Grandpa had made grilled-cheese sandwiches on the wood cookstove for supper, but Sam couldn't eat a bite.

Mom glanced at the kitchen door. "Quiet. Grandpa will hear you. It's only for two weeks. Two weeks out of the whole summer won't hurt you."

Sam slumped in his chair. Two weeks felt like forever. "I don't see why he wants to get to know me now. He never did before."

"Grandpa isn't good with little kids," said Mom. "But now that you're big, the two of you will get along."

Big? Sam was the shortest boy in his grade three class. And the skinniest. "You're no bigger than a tadpole," Grandpa had said when Sam and Mom had arrived at the ranch that afternoon.

"Just follow Grandpa's rules," said Mom, "and you'll be okay."

Sam sighed. Grandpa had explained his rules when he gave Mom and Sam a tour of the ranch.

"Stay away from the machinery," he had said gruffly. "Don't swim in the creek by yourself. Don't feed my dog table scraps. Apart from that, you can do what you want."

What Sam wanted to do was go home.

Grandpa came into the kitchen with an armful of wood for the stove. He was the tallest man Sam had ever seen. He wore blue jeans, dusty cowboy boots and a belt with a huge silver buckle. "Have you got time to see Sam's surprise before you go, Mary?" he said.

Sam's throat felt dry. Mom was leaving right after supper to drive back to the city. She had to be at the airport the next morning to catch a plane to a science conference.

Mom stood up. "A surprise for Sam," she said brightly. "Of course I have time."

"I thought Sam needed a way to get around the ranch," said Grandpa. He stuck a big black cowboy hat on his head. "Come on outside."

It's going to be a bike, thought Sam. Mom must have told Grandpa he had been begging for a new one. Sam perked up as he followed Grandpa and Mom behind the barn.

He gazed around for the bike. A few chickens scratched in the dirt. Grandpa's border collie, Tip, pounced on a mouse in the grass. An enormous white horse in the middle of the corral swished his tail.

No bike.

The horse stretched out his neck and drew back his lips. He had huge yellow teeth.

"His name is Lightning Bolt," said Grandpa. "But I call him Bolt for short."

Bolt was his surprise? Sam's heart plummeted to his feet. Mom said weakly, "He's awfully big."

"Fast too," said Grandpa. "He's old, but he's still got lots of get-up-and-go."

"Maybe a pony would have been better," said Mom.

"Nonsense," said Grandpa. "I hate ponies. Jimmy rode a proper horse from the time he was four years old."

Grandpa was talking about Sam's dad. He died when Sam was a baby. Mom had explained to Sam that Dad had grown up on Grandpa's ranch.

Grandpa chuckled. "Jimmy used to stand on the porch to get on his horse."

Sam shivered. You would need a ladder to get on this horse.

This was the worst surprise he had ever had in his life.

Mom looked at her watch. She said, "I have to go now."

She squeezed Sam tight, but Sam refused to hug her back. He stared at the ground until her car disappeared down the road.

He was alone now—alone with Grandpa and Bolt.

CHAPTER TWO

A REAL COWBOY

The next morning, Sam lay on the bed in the little bedroom that had belonged to Dad. He had woken in the middle of the night because he missed Mom. He felt tired and empty inside. He wished he could have Tip with him, but Grandpa said Tip was a working dog. When Tip was in the house, he had to stay on his blanket in the kitchen.

Horse posters decorated the bedroom walls. Above the dresser hung a framed photograph of a boy standing beside a big brown horse. The boy wore a black cowboy hat like Grandpa's and held a fancy blue ribbon.

The boy must be Dad, thought Sam. He studied the photograph for a long time. Dad must have liked horses a lot.

Sam rolled over on his side. Grandpa had made pancakes for breakfast. Sam had eaten one, but Grandpa had devoured a huge stack with puddles of maple syrup. Then Grandpa and Tip had gone outside, and Sam had gone back to his room.

Grandpa had said as long as he followed the rules, he could do whatever he wanted. If he couldn't go home, Sam decided that what he wanted to do was read. He would read for two whole weeks, and then Mom would be back.

Sam had just dug a book out of his duffel bag when Grandpa appeared in the doorway. He was holding a pair of worn cowboy boots and a black cowboy hat. "These boots belonged to your dad when he was about your size. He called them his lucky boots. And this was his hat. Try them on, and then we'll saddle up that bronc of yours."

Sam felt sick. He had been hoping Grandpa had forgotten all about Bolt. While Grandpa watched, he tugged the boots over his socks. They fit perfectly. He put the hat on. It slid down over his eyes and made him feel mysterious.

"You look like a real cowboy," said Grandpa. "I'll meet you out at the corral in five minutes."

Sam's legs felt like jelly as he trudged out to the corral. Bolt looked even more enormous than he had yesterday. Grandpa had tied him to the fence inside the corral. A wooden crate and a bucket full of brushes sat on the ground. A saddle and a folded blanket rested on the top rail of the fence.

Sam spotted a tall black horse grazing outside the corral. "Is that your horse?" he said. "Are you going to ride too?"

"That's Major," said Grandpa. "He's having the day off today."

Bolt pawed the ground. Sam's heart pounded.

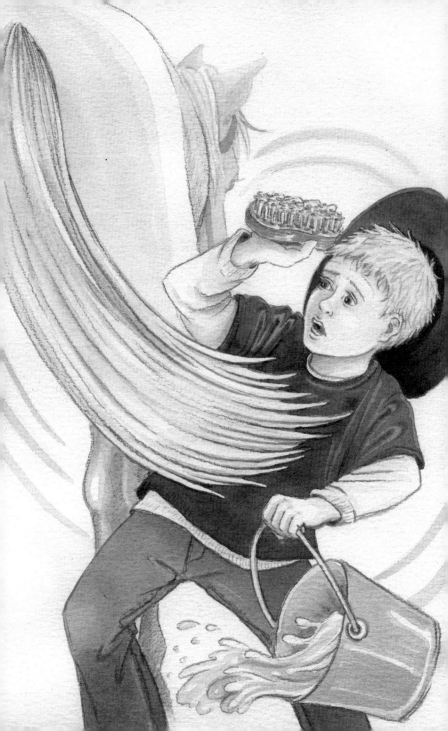

Maybe he should have brought a carrot or something as a peace offering.

Grandpa showed Sam how to brush the dirt off Bolt. Sam took as long as he could. Grandpa turned the wooden crate upside down, and Sam stood on it so he could reach the middle of Bolt's back.

He left Bolt's back legs until the end.

Whoosh! Bolt swished his long tail in Sam's face. "Hey!" cried Sam. He ducked to get out of the way.

"This was your dad's saddle," said Grandpa. He laid the blanket on Bolt's back. He heaved the saddle up and placed it on top of the blanket. The seat was worn and the wooden stirrups were scuffed. He tightened a wide leather strap under Bolt's belly. "Now the bridle. It's a bit tricky until you get used to it. You watch what I do."

The bridle looked like a hopeless tangle of straps and buckles, but in no time Grandpa had it over Bolt's head with the bit clamped in the horse's mouth.

"I'll hoist you up today, but after that you're going to have to figure out your own way to get on," said Grandpa. He swung Sam into the saddle.

Sam held his breath. The ground looked a long, long way down.

"You can't just sit there all day," Grandpa said finally.

Sam slowly let out his breath. What was he supposed to do?

Bolt turned his head and stared at Sam.

"Giddyup," said Sam in a tiny voice.

CHAPTER THREE
SHOW HIM WHO'S BOSS!

"Squeeze with your legs," suggested Grandpa.

Sam gently squeezed the horse's sides. Nothing happened. He squeezed a little harder. With a lurch, Bolt started to walk around the inside of the corral.

Sam yelped and grabbed the saddle horn. Bolt had a bouncy walk. Sam bobbed up and down.

"Sit up straight," said Grandpa. "Look where you're going."

He was going in a big circle. Sam realized with relief that he didn't have to steer. Bolt just followed the fence. All Sam had to do was hold on tight and make sure he didn't fall off.

His shoulders relaxed. Maybe this wasn't going to be so hard after all. He glanced down and admired his boots. Real cowboy boots. Dad's lucky boots.

Bolt came to a sudden stop. Sam flopped forward. The horse lowered his head to a clump of grass in the corner of the corral and grabbed a mouthful.

"Don't let him eat!" roared Grandpa.

Sam tugged on the reins. He couldn't budge Bolt's head. Bolt snatched another mouthful of grass.

"Pull up his head!" said Grandpa.

Sam yanked harder on the reins. "I...can't," he puffed. His face felt hot.

Grandpa snorted. He walked over and slapped Bolt on the rump. Bolt picked up his head and ambled off, grass hanging from his mouth.

"You have to show him you're the boss," said Grandpa.

"Right," muttered Sam.

Round the corral they went. Sam tried to sit up straight. He tried to look where they were going.

He eyed the clump of grass in the corner. The reins strained in his hands as Bolt eyed it too.

Show him you're the boss, thought Sam. He gave Bolt a hard kick and said, "No!"

Bolt burst into a trot. Sam's heart jumped into his throat.

Up and down, up and down, he bounced in the saddle. His feet flew out of the stirrups. The fence and the barn and Grandpa flashed by.

"Whoa!" yelled Sam. "Whoa!"

Grandpa stepped in front of Bolt. He grabbed the reins and pulled Bolt to a stop.

Sam took a huge breath. "I'm getting off!" he said.

He slid off the horse. It was a long way to the ground. His legs wobbled. He thought Grandpa would be disgusted with him.

But Grandpa looked pleased.

"Not bad for your first time," he said. "Tomorrow we'll head out and ride the range."

"Ride the range" was cowboy talk. Sam wasn't exactly sure what it meant. He had a sickening picture in his head of galloping wildly across the fields.

CHAPTER FOUR
MUSCLES OF STEEL

"We need to bring some hay up to the barn for Major and Bolt," said Grandpa. "We'll take the pickup truck."

"Can I ride in the back?" said Sam. He had never ridden in the back of a pickup before.

Grandpa lowered the tailgate, and Sam scrambled in. Tip jumped up beside him. Sam sat down, leaned against the side of the truck and stuck his legs out straight.

Grandpa drove along a bumpy road. The ride was over way too soon. Sam climbed out and gazed around. Golden bales of hay were stacked up in neat rows under a high metal roof.

With both hands, Grandpa grabbed the orange twine wrapped around a bale. He slung the bale into the back of the truck. Sam watched as Grandpa tossed in four more bales.

It looked easy.

Sam wrapped his fingers around the twine on a bale. He tried to sling the bale the way Grandpa did. He couldn't make it budge...not even a tiny bit.

Whew, thought Sam, Grandpa must have muscles of steel. He pulled harder.

Grandpa had stopped lifting bales and was watching him. Sam let his arms drop to his sides. His face felt hot.

Grandpa reached for another bale. But then he stopped, straightened up and rubbed the middle of his back. "These bales are getting heavier every time I come out here," he said. "Maybe you could give me a hand with this last one, Sam."

Sam grabbed one end of the bale and Grandpa grabbed the other. Together they heaved it into the truck.

Sam climbed back in. He perched on top of a hay bale. All around him was the sweet smell of hay. Tip put his front legs up on the bale and licked Sam's hand.

Sam leaned his head back and gazed up at the clear blue sky.

Bump, bump, bump bounced the truck.

Sam could hear Grandpa singing through the open window. For a few seconds, he thought it might be fun to be a cowboy.

Then he remembered Bolt.

CHAPTER FIVE

AN UNEXPECTED BATH

"Do we have to ride the range today?" said Sam.

He was sitting on top of Bolt. Grandpa was sitting on Major.

Grandpa gave Sam a long look. "Not right away," he said. "We're going to my neighbor's house, Doctor McKinnon. She's been my neighbor for forty years. She was your dad's doctor when he was growing up. You'll like her."

Grandpa had put the saddle and bridle on Bolt while Sam watched. Then Grandpa had taken them off and made Sam try to put them back on. It had taken Sam a lot of tries, but finally he got it right.

Then Sam stood on the wooden crate and climbed onto the horse by himself.

He took a deep breath. He was careful to keep his legs still so he wouldn't make Bolt trot again.

"I always go to see Sally McKinnon on Tuesdays," explained Grandpa. He led the way through an open gate into a wide field of rippling grass. "Tuesday is chocolate-chip-cookie day. Sally bakes me a batch of cookies, and I do odd jobs for her in return."

"I love chocolate-chip cookies!" said Sam.

The horses walked across the field, side by side. Tip ran along behind. The tall grass was almost up to Sam's knees. A small brown bird flitted ahead of them, ducking in and out of the grass. A bee hummed.

Grandpa didn't seem to be in a hurry. When they had crossed the field and gone through another open gate, he stopped his horse to show Sam a fox's den. Then he pointed out a gopher sitting in the sun beside a hole in the ground. Tip barked, and the gopher whistled in alarm and disappeared inside the hole.

They rode down a long grassy slope and then along a trail through the forest.

Sam heard the sound of running water. They came out of the trees and stopped in front of a sparkling creek with grassy banks.

"Water's risen a lot since last week," said Grandpa. "All the rain we had." He clucked at his horse. "Come on, Major."

Sam stared in disbelief. They were going to ride across the creek? Grandpa must be crazy. "What about Tip?" he said desperately.

"He loves the water," said Grandpa.

Grandpa rode Major into the creek. Bolt splashed in after them. Sam clung to the saddle horn. The water swirled below his boots. Tip swam past, scrambled out on the opposite bank and gave himself a huge shake.

Midway across the creek, Bolt pulled hard on the reins and lowered his head for a drink. Sam's chest tightened. He thought Grandpa was going to yell at him to stop Bolt. But Grandpa let Major have a drink too. Then Major stepped out of the creek onto the bank.

Bolt lifted his head. "Go," muttered Sam. He didn't like being in the creek by himself.

Bolt stayed where he was. He pawed at the water with his front foot. The spray showered Sam's face.

"Stop!" cried Sam.

Bolt pawed faster and faster. Water splashed everywhere.

Grandpa swung around in his saddle. "That darn horse is going down!" he shouted. "Kick him, Sam!"

Sam remembered what had happened the last time he had kicked Bolt. Sam froze.

Then he felt Bolt's body slowly sink into the water.

Down, down, down.

Icy water rose up the horse's sides. It gushed into Sam's boots. It soaked his jeans.

"Help!" yelled Sam.

Bolt stood up slowly. Water streamed out of Sam's boots. Bolt waded across to the bank. He gave himself a huge shake, just like Tip.

"Hey!" cried Sam. His insides felt scrambled. "What are you doing?"

"Thought you'd take a bath, did you?" said Grandpa. He was grinning.

Sam stared straight ahead. It wasn't funny. He was freezing, and his jeans were stuck to his legs.

For the rest of the way, he didn't talk to Grandpa. They rode along a grassy road until they came to a small white house with a big barn beside it. A gray-haired woman wearing jeans and a blue shirt stood in the doorway of the house.

"Do you think I could hang this boy of mine on your clothesline?" called Grandpa.

CHAPTER SIX

RIDING THE RANGE

"Don't be such a tease, James," said Doctor McKinnon. "I heard you were coming, Sam, and I'm pleased to meet you. We'll sit on the porch in the sun."

Doctor McKinnon brought out a plate of cookies. She and Grandpa sat in two wicker chairs, and Sam sat on the step. He pulled off his boots and his sopping wet socks while Grandpa told his neighbor what had happened.

"I remember the exact same thing happening to your dad, Sam," said Doctor McKinnon.

"It did?" said Sam, shocked. He began to feel a little bit better.

"That horse of his plopped itself right down in the creek. It seems just like yesterday that your dad stood on this porch too, dripping wet."

Grandpa chuckled. "I'd forgotten that. Jimmy was always getting into scrapes."

Sam took a big bite of a chocolate-chip cookie. It was delicious. The sun felt warm on his legs, and already his jeans were starting to dry.

Doctor McKinnon and Grandpa talked about how long the good weather would last for haying and about a cow sale that was coming to town next month. Then Doctor McKinnon told Grandpa about a gate she needed help fixing.

When it was time to go, Doctor McKinnon gave Grandpa a paper bag full of cookies. Grandpa stowed them in his saddlebag.

"Save some of those cookies until you get home," she warned as Grandpa and Sam rode off.

"We're going back a different way," Grandpa said

to Sam. "It takes a lot longer, but there's something I want to show you."

Grandpa and Sam rode past Doctor McKinnon's barn. They rode across a field and through several small groves of trees. They came to the creek again, but at this section there was a sturdy wooden bridge. Sam liked the clumping sound the horse's hooves made on the boards.

After a long time, the trail began to climb up a steep hillside. When they got to the top of the hill, Grandpa stopped.

Below them stretched an ocean of pale green grass. Dotted across the grass were hundreds of black and brown cows.

"Are those all your cows?" gasped Sam.

"Every last one," said Grandpa proudly. "This is their summer range. I'll round them up in the fall."

"By yourself?" said Sam.

"Tip and Major will help me. Tip is a working dog, and Major has good cow sense."

"Cow sense" must be more cowboy talk, thought Sam. He gazed around. He could see for miles and miles. He could see fields, forests and rolling hills.

"Are we riding the range?" he said.

"You bet we are," said Grandpa.

Sam grinned. Riding the range wasn't scary after all. It was kind of fun.

Sam didn't say anything as they rode down the other side of the hill and back into the forest. He was imagining Grandpa and Tip and Major rounding up all those cows.

Crash!

Sam glimpsed something huge and dark charging through the trees. Then *whoosh!* Major and Bolt leaped sideways off the trail.

"Whoa!" yelled Grandpa.

Sam didn't have time to yell. He flew through the air. His cowboy hat sailed off. He landed with a thump on the ground.

Grandpa hopped down off Major. He hurried over to Sam.

"My arm hurts," moaned Sam. "I think it's broken."

A few tears slid down his cheeks. He wiped his face with his shirtsleeve and sat up slowly.

"Let me see if you can move your arm," Grandpa said calmly. "Start with your fingers."

Sam wiggled his fingers back and forth. He didn't want to tell Grandpa his arm wasn't hurting that much now. Grandpa would think he had made a fuss over nothing.

"Was it a bear?" whispered Sam.

Grandpa smiled. "It was a moose. I think it was more startled of us. I'll hoist you up."

Sam put his cowboy hat back on. He looked at Bolt. His heart started to pound. He took a big breath.

"I'm not getting on," he said in a loud voice. "I'm never riding again."

CHAPTER SEVEN

A LONG WALK

"A cowboy always gets back on his horse when he falls off," said Grandpa.

"I'm not a cowboy," said Sam. "And I'm not getting on."

Grandpa's eyebrow twitched. "How are you going to get home?"

"I'll walk," said Sam.

Grandpa sighed. "Suit yourself. But it's a long way."

Grandpa held on to Bolt's lead rope and clucked at Major. They started walking down the trail. Grandpa didn't look back.

He doesn't care, thought Sam. He felt flushed. He hurried to catch up. It was hard to walk on the rough trail in cowboy boots. He wished he had his runners on. Then he could run all the way home.

When they had been walking for a long time, Grandpa turned around and said, "Change your mind?"

"No," said Sam stiffly.

By the time they got back to the corral, Sam was hot and tired. His legs ached. He had blisters on both heels. He started toward the house, but Grandpa said, "Wait a minute. A cowboy always looks after his horse first."

"That wasn't one of your stupid rules!" Sam burst out.

"It's one of my rules now," said Grandpa.

Sam took one look at Grandpa's face. Then he muttered, "Fine."

He waited while Grandpa took the saddle and bridle off Bolt. Then he brushed the sweat and dust off the horse. He carried the saddle and bridle into the barn, and put the saddle on its rack and the bridle on a hook. Then he let Bolt loose in the corral with Major.

Sam stormed into the house. He sped upstairs to his bedroom and slammed the door.

He hated being a cowboy! And he hated Grandpa!

He lay on his bed and stared at the ceiling for a long time. Finally he drifted asleep, and when he woke up the light outside had faded.

There was a knock on the door, and Grandpa said, "Supper is ready."

Sam didn't answer. He waited until Grandpa's footsteps had gone away, and then he got out his book. The book had seemed interesting before, but now it was boring. He sighed and put it down.

For a while there had been noises coming from downstairs—pots and pans banging, the thump of wood being loaded into the stove, water running. Now there was silence.

Sam opened the door. The smell of hamburgers cooking made his stomach rumble. He tiptoed to the

top of the stairs. Tip sat at the bottom of the stairs, staring up at him.

Sam sucked in his breath. Had Tip forgotten Grandpa's rule about staying on his blanket?

"Here, Tip," said Sam softly. "Come on, boy."

Tip tilted his head, and then he bounded up the stairs. Sam pushed him into the bedroom and shut the door firmly behind them.

Tip explored Sam's heap of clothes on the floor and the inside of the closet. Then he hopped up on the bed and curled into a ball.

Sam searched in his duffel bag for two of the granola bars Mom had packed in case he got hungry at night. He tore off the wrappers. He gave one bar to Tip, who gulped it down in three big bites. Sam gobbled down the second bar. He lay down on the bed and put his hand on the dog's soft back.

Sam was just dozing off again when he heard his door open. He closed his eyes and pretended to be asleep.

"Hey," said Grandpa, "so that's what you're up to, Tip."

Sam held his breath. He felt the dog stir beside him.

And then Grandpa said softly, "It's okay, Tip. You stay right there tonight."

Sam let out a big sigh as the bedroom door clicked shut.

CHAPTER EIGHT

STORM!

A loud noise woke Sam in the middle of the night.

Thunder!

He climbed out of bed and went to the window.

Lightning zigzagged across the sky. Thunder rumbled. Wind howled and rattled his window.

Tip whined. Sam shivered. Grandpa's house was old. It felt like it was going to blow right over.

"Come on, Tip," said Sam. "Let's find Grandpa."

Grandpa was standing at the kitchen window. "It's a dandy of a storm," he said. "Come and have a look."

Grandpa didn't sound worried. Sam stood beside him. Lightning flashed, and huge tree branches swayed back and forth.

"Power will go out if this keeps up," said Grandpa. "But I've brought in lots of wood for the stove. We'll be safe and snug inside."

"What about Bolt and Major?" said Sam. "What about all the cows?"

"I put the horses in the barn," said Grandpa. "I could feel this storm coming. And a bit of bad weather won't hurt those cows. They'll hunker down."

Sam was glad he wasn't a cow. He was glad he was watching the storm from inside the house.

His stomach rumbled. "I'm hungry," he said.

"I was just going to suggest hot chocolate," said Grandpa. "And maybe a warmed-up hamburger."

Sam sipped his hot chocolate while Grandpa heated the hamburger in a frying pan on the woodstove. He had just finished eating when the lights blinked off.

Grandpa had flashlights ready. "A big tree must have fallen down somewhere," he said. "Knocked out the lines. We'll go back to bed, and then we'll see what has to be done in the morning."

When Sam stood up, Tip stood up too. Sam held his breath. He thought the storm wouldn't be so scary if Tip could stay with him.

Grandpa didn't say anything when Tip followed Sam upstairs. Tip jumped up onto the end of Sam's bed. Sam pulled the covers right up to his chin.

Crash! The thunder sounded like it was on top of them. Tip inched his way closer to Sam. Sam rubbed his ears. "Good boy," he said. "Good boy."

When Sam woke up, it was morning. Tip was gone.

Sam scrambled out of bed and ran to the window. The ground below was littered with fallen branches, but the wind had stopped.

Sam found Grandpa and Tip in the kitchen. "Is the power still out?" said Sam.

Grandpa was frying eggs. "Yup. The phone lines are down too. But the storm has passed by. There's just some cleanup to do now."

Sam dove into his eggs.

"I already ate," said Grandpa. "While you finish up your breakfast, Tip and I'll go outside and have a look around. See if there's any damage."

Sam ate every last bite and put his plate in the sink. He walked around the house, peering out all the windows. There were tree branches lying everywhere on the ground.

Grandpa had been gone a long time. Sam went to the door. He could hear Tip barking. He frowned. Tip sounded frantic.

Sam stepped outside. He gazed around. Then his heart gave a huge jump. Grandpa lay on the ground beside a tall evergreen tree. A thick tree limb lay across his chest. Tip stood next to him, barking shrilly.

"Grandpa!" shouted Sam.

CHAPTER NINE

A FAST RIDE

Sam ran over to Grandpa. Grandpa's face was gray. Blood seeped from a cut on his forehead.

His lips moved, and Sam bent closer.

"Darn branch...wind broke it off," mumbled Grandpa. "Hanging in that tree...fell down and hit me on the head."

Sam tugged at the branch. It was heavy, but he managed to pull it off.

Grandpa tried to stand up. Then he sank back to the ground. "Feel kind of dizzy," he said. "Best if I stay here for a while."

He closed his eyes.

"What should I do?" said Sam.

But Grandpa didn't answer him.

"Grandpa!" cried Sam. "Grandpa!"

Grandpa's eyes stayed shut.

Sam's heart pounded. "Don't worry, Grandpa," he said. "I'll get help!"

Sam was a fast runner. But he didn't know if he could run all the way to Doctor McKinnon's house.

He thought of Bolt.

Sam's heart thudded. He needed Dad's lucky boots. He flew to the house. He pulled the boots on, jammed his cowboy hat on his head and grabbed a blanket off Grandpa's bed.

Sam ran back to Grandpa. He tucked the blanket around Grandpa's shoulders.

Tip's brown eyes looked worried. "You stay here, Tip," said Sam. "You look after Grandpa."

Sam raced to the barn.

Bolt and Major were in their stalls, eating. Bolt looked up with interest at Sam.

"You gotta help me, Bolt," said Sam. "We've gotta save Grandpa."

Sam set the wooden crate upside down in the stall beside Bolt. Then he got the saddle and the blanket. He threw the blanket over Bolt's back. He climbed up on the crate with the saddle and heaved it on top of the blanket. He tightened the leather girth.

Sam picked up Bolt's bridle. Grandpa made it look so easy, but it wasn't. There were straps and buckles everywhere. Sam's hands shook as he slid the bridle over Bolt's head. Bolt opened his mouth, and Sam slipped the bit between his teeth.

Bolt was ready. Sam's heart pounded as he led the horse outside the barn. He ran back for the crate and put it beside Bolt. Then he climbed onto the horse's back.

Sam didn't want to go through the creek again. But it was the shortest way to Doctor McKinnon's house.

He rode Bolt through the open gate into the field. He held on to the saddle horn and kicked Bolt's sides.

Bolt started to trot. Sam bounced up and down. But he didn't fall off.

Across the field they trotted. Down the long grassy slope and along the trail through the forest.

A deer bounded through the trees, and Bolt jumped. Sam clung on tightly.

When they came to the creek, Sam's stomach tightened. But Bolt splashed right through without stopping.

Sam leaned over and patted Bolt's neck. "Good boy," he said.

Up the grassy road they trotted. Bolt didn't stop until he got to Doctor McKinnon's house.

Sam slid off the horse's back. His legs felt weak.

"Doctor McKinnon!" he yelled. "Grandpa's hurt!"

CHAPTER TEN
SAM'S PROMISE

Doctor McKinnon knew just what to do. She put Bolt in her barn. Then she and Sam got in her truck and drove to Grandpa's ranch.

Doctor McKinnon and Sam climbed out of the truck and hurried over to Grandpa. Grandpa was sitting up, leaning against the tree. His eyes were open, but his face was white. Tip was lying beside him. He jumped up and barked.

"How did you know to come?" said Grandpa to Doctor McKinnon.

"Sam got me," said Doctor McKinnon in a matter-of-fact voice. "He rode Bolt over to my house."

Grandpa didn't look surprised. He said, "That boy of mine. He's something else."

Sam thought Grandpa was talking about Dad again. Until Grandpa looked right at him and said, "Thank you, Sam."

"You're welcome," mumbled Sam.

Doctor McKinnon peered at Grandpa's forehead. "That's a nasty cut, and I'll bet you'll end up with a big goose egg. It's a good thing Sam got me. You're going to need stitches."

"Now, now, don't fuss," protested Grandpa weakly.

"I'm not fussing," said Doctor McKinnon. "I'm telling you straight. Sam and I are going to get you into my truck, and we're going to the hospital. The doctors will need to check for a concussion too."

Sam and Doctor McKinnon each took one of Grandpa's arms and helped him walk to the truck. Once Grandpa was settled in the front seat with a blanket over his shoulders, Sam scrambled into the backseat.

"Don't forget Tip," said Grandpa. "He'll fret if he's left alone."

Tip jumped into the truck. Sam petted the dog, who curled up beside him.

"Now don't you worry about anything, Sam," said Doctor McKinnon as they headed down the road. "Your Grandpa is a tough nut. He'll be back in the saddle in a week."

Sam leaned forward. "Grandpa, do you think Bolt has good cow sense?"

"Well, now, I know he does," said Grandpa.

"Can I come back in the fall and help you round up the cows?"

Sam held his breath. Grandpa turned around in his seat. His face was lit up with a huge smile.

"You better make that a promise," he said. "I'll need a good cowboy."

"I promise," said Sam.